D1443816

JACK LONDON'S DOG

Dirk Wales

JACK LONDON'S DOG

Illustrated by Barry Moser

GREAT PLAINS PRESS · CHICAGO 2008

A Great Plains Press Publication

Text copyright ©, Dirk Wales, 2008
Illustrations copyright ©, Barry Moser, 2008

Typeset in the United States by Barry Moser
Printed and bound in China through AsiaPacificOffset

This book is dedicated to Jack London and the dog he knew
in the Yukon during the Gold Rush of 1897.
The dog was also named Jack, and six years later
he would become the fictional Buck, mythic dog of
Call of the Wild.

We know what happened to Jack London, Buck,
and *Call of the Wild*. This story is about what
might have happened to Jack, the dog
who was left behind.

THE YUKON

IMAGINE GETTING YOURSELF as well as the necessary food and equipment from San Francisco harbour to Dawson City in the Yukon in 1897. First you boarded a ship in any city along the American west coast and sailed to Seattle and changed ships or sailed directly to Skagway, at the bottom of the Yukon. From there, men and equipment struggled to get beyond the legendary Chilcoot Pass which stood as a 3600 foot sentinel guarding the precious gold country from man.

After crossing the Pass with heavy gold panning equipment and the food necessary to sustain body and soul, you had only to row handmade boats and walk the next almost 600 miles to Dawson City.

This journey is the definition of Gold Fever.

GULF OF ALASKA

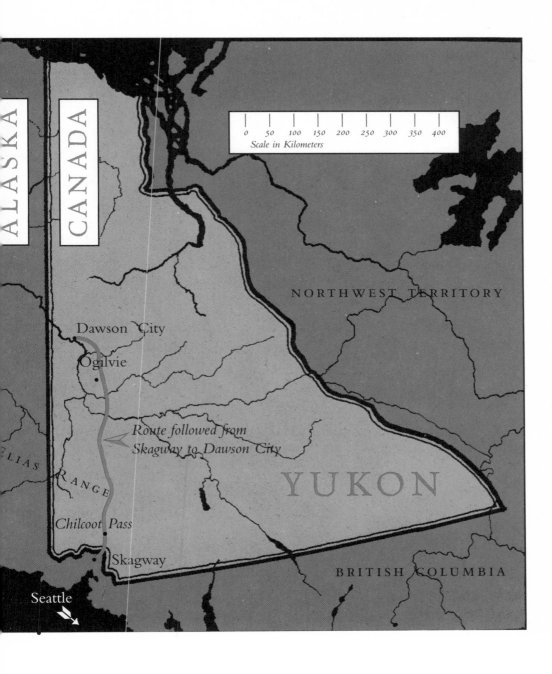

ALASKA

CANADA

0 50 100 150 200 250 300 350 400
Scale in Kilometers

NORTHWEST TERRITORY

Dawson City

Ogilvie

Route followed from
Skagway to Dawson City

ELIAS

RANGE

YUKON

Chilcoot Pass

Skagway

Seattle

BRITISH COLUMBIA

IT WAS A CRISP SUNNY DAY on Split Up Island. Two dogs, Jack and Nic, were sleeping on the porch.

Jack woke up suddenly and looked around. It was quiet, which meant that the men had gone again to Dawson to stake more claims for land along the river—the river that was supposed to yield gold to them after the thaw.

Jack's master then was Marshall Bond, one of the men who lived on Split Up Island waiting for winter to be over and the gold mining to begin. For all in the North, it was an unstable time, so it was common for a dog to have many masters. No one knows where Jack lived, or with whom, before his time in the Yukon.

Now Jack's nose pulled him to his feet. His nose led him around the island as if it were a rope pulled by an invisible force. He walked into the slight wind, caught the scent, and followed it to the place along the river between two trees.

He dug there in the snow and within a foot or so found what delighted his nose memory—a delicious bone. Though his nose memory led him there, the other part of his memory could not say when he had buried it. No matter, the bone was here now and was as delicious as a bone should be.

When the men returned to Split Up Island, they fed the dogs, but Jack didn't eat much, and his master, Marshall Bond, wondered out loud if Jack was fit. A man had to see to his dogs in this country. It was dog and man against everything else in the white wilderness. Jack was popular with the other men, so along with Marshall Bond they watched the dog to see if he was fit. The men nodded.

He was fit.

❧ THERE WERE TWO KINDS of dogs in the Klondike during the rush for gold, a rush where a hundred thousand men sought the yellow dust and nuggets along the rivers that flowed into the Yukon River.

One kind of dog was "outsider." The other was "insider." Huskies and almost-wolves were "insider" dogs, born to the North Country. They were sleek and hardy dogs who could live with the laws of raw nature. They were born to wildness, so they had to be tamed only to the ways of man.

"Outsider" dogs were brought to the Klondike from the West Coast towns south of Alaska. They had to learn the lore of the North, of bitter weather and mistreatment, of hard labor pulling the loads of equipment needed to seek the precious gold. Life could be mean for a dog like this.

❧ ONE DAY A SMALL BOAT came upriver with three strange men. Like all men along the Yukon River in 1897, they came for the gold. But the freeze-up had come and it was too late to pan for gold this year. They would have to wait 'til the thaw. Jack London got out of the boat and talked with the men of Split Up Island. They said London and his two companions could stay with them on the Island for the winter.

Jack the dog walked up to Jack London and sniffed him. London reached down and put his hands deeply into the dog's fur. The man's hands felt good to the dog, and he smelled right.

12

THERE WAS LITTLE FOR the men to do on Split Up Island during the winter except dream of gold and the riches it would bring. They thought of nothing else, yet they had to live in the meantime. Some men cooked for the group. Other men gathered firewood for warmth in the hearth of each cabin. Trees had to be cut down and chopped into pieces that would fit into the fireplaces. The cooking was done in these same fireplaces, so they were large for cooking and for providing heat to each cabin. No one knows exactly how many men lived on the Island that winter, only that they thought and planned and hoped constantly for the thaw and the time when they could dig and pan for the precious gold they so desired. Then they would be rich, they thought.

Much of the planning meant the men had to pore over maps of Dawson City, the area around it, and the river that flowed through. Often they would take a boat and explore parts of the river where they guessed gold might be. At night, they would argue over supper about the best places to try for gold. Once a decision was made, they would travel to Dawson to place a "claim" for a certain section of land, usually along the river, where they would—once the thaw came—find the precious gold. The Dream of Gold was a finely tailored and ornately dressed idea firmly held in the mind and heart of each man. Once the Yukon had made them rich, why, then they could return to their homes all over North America. Some men even came from France, like Jacques, or from Mexico, like Mendez. These men had families or girlfriends back home. They had left these homes plain men. When they returned, they would be rich and treated like kings. They would be regarded as special men who had adventured and risked all in the treacherous North Country, where the cold and the dangers killed men and dogs alike.

What a feeling that would be!

THE TWO JACKS BECAME friends. They did many things together. One day in Dawson, where they had gone upriver, Jack and London became separated. London had gone inside an office to sign some papers. He did not notice that the dog had wandered off, distracted by some nearby horses. London did not realize that Jack was interested in horses and wanted to get close enough to smell them. There were few horses in the North Country. They were a curious new smell for Jack. Horses were big and could kick, as Jack saw when another dog got too close to the hooves of a gray horse.

14

Forgetting his master for a moment, Jack wandered off to the far end of Dawson where there were even more interesting smells. Suddenly the dog missed his master. He looked around and saw that he was far from familiar landmarks and the smell of London's trousers. His nostrils flared and he used his memory of London's scent to search him out. When he got near to the door of the office London had gone into, he was distracted by a horse who suddenly shied and bucked. The horse wheeled and began racing down the street.

Directly in the horse's path stood Jack London. With no time to think, the dog leaped with all his might at the racing horse. It was as if two arrows had been shot at the same moment—horse and dog on a collision path. Jack's forepaws hit the back of the horse's head and threw him off his path. London, seeing the danger, jumped to the side. Dog and horse fell away into a mess over a wooden sidewalk.

15

London pulled himself up and walked over to where Jack lay alongside the horse, who was snorting wildly. London led the dog away from the crowd of men that gathered to see the ruckus. Finally, he stopped and pushed his hands and face deep into Jack's fur. It was a quiet moment between man and dog. Each felt the strong bond as if there was shared blood.

Later that day in Dawson, Jack London fed Jack the best pan of stew he had ever eaten. London sat in the street and watched him eat the stew. Afterward, he petted Jack. Often on Split Up Island the dog would remember this day in Dawson with the man he thought of as his real master.

BACK AT THE CABIN Jack often sat at the feet of his friend, Jack London, while the other men sat at the fire and told London their stories. There were many men and many stories. There was a writer hidden deep inside Jack London, and that writer was collecting fuel for the stories he would write in years to come about this place and these times. He had a powerful memory. He would remember.

There were stories of the white wilderness, of men who were caught in it and did not survive, and stories of men caught in it yet living to tell the tale this night in front of the fire. There were stories of dogsleds, of icy rivers, of gold and death. Once there was even a story of men carrying sacks of gold dust worth a hundred thousand dollars out of the North Country. A hundred thousand dollars of gold dust in 1897 would be worth millions years later. But these millions were nothing compared to the excitement of the dreams of men and nature caught up in the harsh North Country. Most of all, there were stories of their loyal dogs, dogs who would live forever in the future of London's stories.

During these storytelling times Jack would lie on the floor in front of the fire and think about his life in the North Country, where men could be

16

greedy and mean. It was a hard life for a dog, but it was good, too. He thought about how he had saved his master's life. Jack was glad there were not very many horses in the Yukon, but he wondered what other challenges lay ahead. He was glad that Jack London lived on Split Up Island and would hunt gold with him in the wild North Country.

EACH NIGHT THE MEN lay under blankets and furs and dreamed their dreams of gold. Who is to say that dogs don't dream as well? On this night, London and Jack went to sleep together. London lay down on a wooden rack comforted by many furs. The dog, too big for the rack, lay down nearby on an old blanket. As soon as the warmth crept into their bones, they fell into a dream… they are on top of a ridgeline across the river. Below them, off to the west, appears a pack of wolves. The wolves form a grayish line along the bottom of the valley, a moving line that wavers and thins and loses itself in the tree line and then emerges like an arrow, pointed and dangerous.

17

The eyes of London and the dog are just far enough away not to see what the wolves see—three deer standing in a line of young saplings. On command, the wolves divide themselves into a circling line, half this way, half that way, curving until they surround the deer. London is bewildered. He has never in his waking life seen anything like this. He looks down to see if Jack understands. Neither of them knows how wolves run down deer.

They watch and learn.

Breaking the circle, the leader of the pack attacks first, with two wolves behind him. The deer quickly bolt in the opposite direction. Just as they gain enough speed to outrun the point of the arrow, they run into the net of wolves waiting for them. The deer are at once surrounded by a mass of open jaws. One deer heels, turns abruptly, and, free of the net, is followed hopelessly by a jagged group of wolves until they can no longer keep pace, and they turn back, leaving this deer to be the only survivor of the afternoon. By the time the small pack returns to the main kill, the two deer are down, and all the wolves join the feast.

London, stunned, thinking that Jack can hear him and perhaps even respond, says under his breath, "If this deathly place had a form of poetry, we have just seen it. As if life itself and death were dancing partners, whirling in the white silence—even at this short distance, we heard nothing. It was all a dumb show, all a racing action, a race in which one lives and two die so that the pack can be nourished in a land where fallen snow cannot grow, thrive, nor feed. Only the earth under the snowpack will survive to nourish leaves at the ends of branches come spring."

In the dream, Jack looks up at the man, ears perked. London falls to his knees and puts his hand heavily on the dog's head and weeps. It is not cold enough for the tears to freeze before they drop onto Jack's fur.

"We better be getting back down to the river and row ourselves home for supper," London says. Jack licks a tear from the man's cheek. Then they get

18

up and turn to the river, down to the boat and across to Split Up Island, safe from the raw white harshness. . . .

In the hushed darkness of the cabin, the fire in the far corner lit London's waking face. He shook himself and looked down at the dog and touched him. His friend, Jack, was there, looking up at him, both awake, both wondering what had happened in the other's dream.

❧ ONE PARTICULARLY COLD MORNING, Jack London got up and dressed in the warmest clothes he could find. Through the log walls of the cabin he could sense that this could be the coldest of days. Cold, cold, he thought.

He opened the door and his breath almost choked him. He turned his face inside, breathing, and then outside, almost breathing, back and forth until he felt he could walk outside the cabin and continue to breathe.

There was no thermometer—no way to know what degree of cold it was.

He had heard men speak of winter days with no sun, when the thermometer dropped below zero, fifty degrees below or even more. He recalled one night in front of a fire, and just the thought of the flames warmed him. His friend Dutch had told him about being out in the freeze and it was that cold—fifty degrees below zero. Dutch had said the only thing that saved him was that another man had asked to travel with him. It took the two of them working together to build the lifesaving fires along the trail. The freeze was so deep and dangerous that they dared not sleep for fear of never waking up—they stayed sleepless and fearful until they reached the safety and warmth of Dawson.

London walked to the edge of the Island, then one hundred fifty-odd yards to the other side of the river. He walked those banks, thinking. . . imagine being able to walk across a river, where had there been water, he would have been swept away in the current. Imagine being eighty degrees away from

19

what a cold day would be in his hometown of Oakland, California, and the San Francisco Bay!

What kind of a place is this?

He picked his way through the iron snow, frozen brush, and broken trees—trees exploded by the cold. How can man exist here? An answer came to his mind, and he tried to shake it out of his head. Is it that man can exist here only by becoming as harsh and extreme as the land and the weather and the white silence all around? That would make this country the most dangerous and wildest in existence, surely. Surely it would.

He turned back to the shelter of the Island cabin and the fire before his nature turned as cold as that around him. What kind of man might he be should that happen? His heart shuddered.

WHEN THE THAW CAME and the snow thinned it was time to pan for the gold the men lusted for. But Jack London put his hands deeply into his dog friend's fur and stroked him for the last time. London was sick and had to return south to his home in Oakland, California, to recover.

The dog didn't understand that this would be the last time. London had gone away in the boat and returned many times. But this time there would be no return. Even Jack London did not realize he would never see the North Country again. But he would relive these experiences hundreds of times, as if they were sacks of gold to be exchanged for pages in books and dollars in years to come. He would indeed strike it rich, but in a warmer, gentler place. Had someone on the banks of Split Up Island said that, all surely would have laughed.

For weeks after, Jack stood on the bank of the Yukon River looking upstream for his friend Jack London to come home, come back to put his hands on him, come back so Jack could smell his trousers. On days like this, Jack would lick his paws and whine. He was a sad dog.

20

After many weeks, Jack knew that his master would not return, though he did not understand why. What Jack had yet to learn was that life shifted, that it was necessary to be ready for change and make the best of it.

THERE WERE MANY RIVER forks in the Yukon. Different paths led to surprising places for both man and dog. After the thaw came, after Jack London left and the business of all living in the Yukon was gold, the path was difficult, littered with greedy men and hard-working dogs. The bright sunlight of summer had its harsh shadows. This is not to say that there were not good men as well as bad, but Jack was to have a bad master.

Franco Stupendo believed that there was gold not only in Dawson City and the surrounding rivers but also in the rivers across the mountain. One nightfall at Split Up Island, two of Franco's brothers, moving like shadows in the dark, spied Jack and another dog, knocked them out, and hauled them into their boat and away.

It was so quick—the dogs were unconscious—that there was no sound to the theft; no one knew until morning that the two dogs were missing.

Where could they be?

A late spring gale hit Franco, his brothers, and their dogs at the top of the pass. As the wind whipped and tore at the tents, one of the dogs, Jinx, tried to escape from the tent. The ripping sound made all of them crazy. Mario

22

and Tony began quarreling, and Mario tore his brother's cheek with his wolf ring. Mario had paid a great deal of money for this ring in Dawson, thinking that such a ring would bring him good luck finding gold and later, back home, a beautiful wife.

In the treacherous pass that day, the ring brought Mario bad luck, as Tony gave a tremendous blow to Mario's chest, knocking him out. Franco and Jack stood back in the tent watching the fight, listening to the tearing of men and wind. Jinx calmed himself by licking Mario's wounds and whining.

The three brothers roused themselves after the storm and worked their way down out of the high country pass to a river they thought might contain gold. While crossing that rushing river, Army and Sut, two of the trail dogs, got into a scrap on the barge carrying them over the river. Army, bloodied from the fight, slipped and fell into the river. Jack was quick and grabbed Army's tail and held him fast to the edge of the boat, but Mario clubbed Jack back. Jack lost his grip on Army's tail. Army yelped as he flowed downriver with the current until he disappeared from sight. Jack watched his friend drown in the white water.

That night Jack curled by the fire and dreamed of Jack London and how he might return to save both Army and Jack from these three brothers who seemed mad for gold. How London would fight the men and bloody them as the dogs had been bloodied. And how Jack would be reunited with his friend, going off together in the wild, taking care of each other, becoming safe.

❧ HUNGER AND MORE HARDSHIP closed in on the three brothers and their dogs.

There was not enough food, so the dogs were not fed. There was much work during the day as the brothers harnessed the dogs to clear rocks from the creek bed to seek gold. Amee, the lead dog, lost a foot in this endeavor.

As the brothers hitched the dogs to move a huge fallen tree, a stranger walked into their camp. The brothers shunned the stranger, thinking that he would try to take gold from them. They had already gathered a small cache of yellow pebbles.

The stranger saw that the dogs were hungry. He pulled beef jerky out of his pack to feed Jack, Amee, and Lee Lou. The brothers said nothing while the stranger fed their dogs. They watched him carefully. He watched them carefully. Along the river all were animals who could not speak, but only watch.

❧ THIS SAME DAY, Jack London writes at his desk in Oakland, California. He is writing about the North Country. His hands are clean, his hair is combed, and he looks like a civilized man. He is writing a story about the men and dogs he met caught in the white silence of the Yukon. He is writing this in a comfortable room. A cup of dark coffee steams beside him.

His memory clear, he remembers every detail, every man he met, every story they told of their struggle for gold, their dreams of going home to beautiful women with sacks of this gold, of their striving to stay alive, always fighting the cold nature of men or the elements. He remembers also the times on Split Up Island, in Dawson, and in the wild whiteness of the raw

24

North. In particular, he remembers Jack, the dog who loved him.

He writes and writes and writes.

A DISAGREEMENT AROSE between the stranger, whose name was Jake Jamison, and the brothers. The stranger claimed that this dog, he points to Jack, was his—that this dog was stolen from him near the Yukon River. The brothers answer that they were never on the Yukon River. Tony shouted "Lies!" The dogs barked and circled around while the two men struggled, and the brothers, seeing this, did not interfere. Jamison knocked Tony Stupendo down. Tony knocked Jamison down. The dogs secretly wanted Jamison to win, for he fed them and seemed to be a kinder man than the brothers. The dogs yipped and howled during the fight while the two brothers remained calm, believing their brother would win the fight. Then Jamison knocked Tony Stupendo down unconscious. He moved quickly to Jack, knife in hand. He cut Jack from his lead and walked out of the camp with him.

The two cursing brothers tended to Tony. The other dogs watched and whined as Jack was led away. They knew what was in store for them now.

Jack looked back at the camp where he had been living and at the dogs who were his brothers for a time. He looked up at Jamison and knew that this man saved his life, that eventually he would have drowned, or lost a paw like Amee, or even starved to death as the three brothers went mad for gold.

25

Jack's step quickened. He did not care where the trail led now that he was with this stranger who seemed to be like his friend Jack London.

The dog looked up at the mountain. The sun seemed warmer today.

A MAN WEARING A suit and tie sits at a desk in San Francisco. On his desk lies a sheaf of papers. In one hand he holds the pipe he is smoking; in the other he is holding more pages from the story on his desk.

The man nods and says to Jack London, who is standing near the desk, "I like your story. What a time that must have been, eh, London? You in the wild North. Mighty fine. I'll publish this story in my magazine. I like it."

Jack London is happy. He is becoming the writer he always wanted to be. He is becoming known as a man who writes fine adventure stories about that Gold Rush back in '97.

THE DOG JACK FELT a hypnotic effect traveling in the North Country. The bonding of the good man and dog happened easily, as if they were family. Their way of life, always together, always dependent on each other, made them good family rather than bad family, like the Stupendo brothers. Good families or bad families were what life was about for dog and man. And there was no more talk of gold.

This white timelessness was created in part by the isolation of the North Country. There were villages and small towns like Dawson, but mainly there were valleys, mountains, streams, trees, and sometimes other animals like the swift snowshoe rabbit, who was often seen and, if a man was quicker, often eaten. There were bears, but Jack had not seen one in a long time. One night, over the campfire, Jamison had been talking—it was his habit to talk often to Jack—and his soft voice soothed the dog. Jamison began telling Jack about the bear that had almost killed him. How the bear had Jamison down and

26

mauled him with its huge paws. How at the very last minute, Jamison gathered all his strength and turned his body away from the bear and laid a hand on his camp spade, a small shovel with a sharp point, and thrust it into the bear. Jamison's good luck, he said, was that he hit the bear square in the throat, and the bear collapsed, spouting blood like a river. The poor luck of the moment was that the dead bear fell on him. Without a companion to help, it took Jamison over an hour to free himself. But then he had the bear to himself, to eat, skin, and make a fine blanket. Jamison patted what they were lying on.

"This is that same old fellow," he said.

It pleased Jack when Jamison talked to him. His friend Jack London had talked to him as well, and it gave him a good feeling. He looked up into the face of his master and, in the light from the fire he saw something on the neck of the man he had not noticed before. Paw marks. He looked at the marks on the man's neck and then looked down at his own paw. The marks were much larger than his paws, so, thought Jack, an animal three times his own size.

Jamison was looking into the fire now, not under the bear nor over the bear, but alive and breathing. His eyes were deep in his head, and his mouth was soft and thin. The man looked back at the dog and smiled and nodded. His eyes were like the blue river when he did that, and in this way, Jack knew that the man and he were, well, not like litter mates, but surely family, if a man and a dog can be such.

A GREAT AMOUNT OF water surrounded Jack London's home in Oakland, California. Across the Bay from him is the great city of San Francisco. Yet sometimes he longs for smaller water, a river, like the Yukon River near Dawson City in the gold country.

He thinks now of his time there, of how the men and dogs and the raw country of the North might make a fine story for him to write. finally, he recalls smaller water, the American River that flows into the great Bay of San Francisco. He goes there late one afternoon. He sits on the edge of a pier jutting into the water. He reaches down to the water. It is not freezing cold. He watches the sun set in the West.

He thinks now, deeply, of those times. They seem to call to him, and he thinks to answer that call. What will he say?

Perhaps he needs to come often to this river and think more.

THE SUN WAS CRACKING up over the late snow along the mountain edge over the river gorge. The river was thin, but the gorge was deep. There had been a late snowfall—twenty or thirty inches on the banks of the river.

28

Jamison and Jack made camp before the snowfall in the night. Now their tent was covered, buried. Jack woke and looked for his master, but he was not in the tent. Jack got up and nosed his way up and out of the tent into the sunshine. The man was not to be seen. Jack walked through the deep snow following with his nose the faint footprints. He walked to the edge of the river thinking that the man would be there. He might have gone to break ice for water, to make his strong-smelling black liquid, as he did every morning and evening camp.

He was not by the river.

He was not to be seen.

Jack put his nose to the wind. . . .

. . . he followed the scent of the man's boots in the tracks until it was obscured by the blowing wind moving the top layer of snow. Then the wind shifted and Jack sensed he had gone too far. Where there was no scent but the chill biting air before, now Jack nosed down, almost scraping the surface of the snowpack. Here he scented the deep heat of the earth, hoping that it might be mixed with the heated smell of the man. Slowly he turned back, retracing his own pawprints. Moving, moving slowly, until finally he gained a scent that might be his master. He turned his head to gain direction. The slight scent of Jamison was coming again, slowly, and Jack moved inches at a time now, instinctively turning upriver in the direction of the scent from below that seemed to come from his master.

The tent was off in the distance. Ahead, the smell of the man became stronger and stronger—pulling his nose deeper and deeper down into the snow. Jack did not notice as he moved upriver that the banks of snow were deeper here, that he could now look down off to his left where the water still ran quickly, a glistening white thread in the wilderness. He continued upslope, following his nose.

29

30

Jack stopped, sat, and inhaled. He is here, Jack thought, underneath me. He wondered how that might be, that his master was buried under the snow. Bones, not men, were buried under the snow.

A WOMAN HOLDS A book in her warm hand. The book title faces away from her, toward the man who stands in front of her, Jack London. The title of the book is *Son of the Wolf.*

The woman looks happy. Jack London is smiling, too. It is easier now for him to think of himself as a writer—all those printed pages, all those stories of men and wolves and trails in the white silence of the North Country.

DOGPAWS LIKE WINDMILLS whirling into the whiteness of the snow. Jack became something unrecognized, a force so strong that sense and feeling and sight lost their meaning. The dog was caught in the rapture of snatching life from death, an idea that his old friend Jack London would surely have understood. Jack dug furiously into the packed snow in the sure knowledge that because scent was below, there would also be breath, and he would find it. The surest knowledge—that of rock and bone, of spine and tree, of hammer and head—the surest knowledge was his, and there it was, as if he were pawing aside a cloud of fog and all was revealed. Closer and closer, he knew it now, beneath his paws was the man he searched for. His first contact was on his upper body, perhaps his head, and Jack fought to pull his claws in toward his own breath and lead with the fur of his paws, as tenderly as he knew how, though he did not know how. He unearthed his master as if he were a human island beneath a white ocean.

Jack popped out of the snow onto the surface with the amazed Jamison. Had he been asked before the event what he would do faced with such a vision, Jamison would surely have said he would shout to God in thanks, but when the moment came, he simply touched the dog as if to test the reality

31

of this world: it was his dog, his hand touching his dog who had pulled him out of the white jaws of death. Jamison looked into the warm eyes of his friend, who would do anything for his master.

Amen.

After this ordeal, both man and dog were exhausted. They lay together alongside the open white wound and tried to breathe normally. Jamison's hand lay on Jack's crusty fur. It was as though a new connection had opened between them, the one saved and the savior. Finally, Jamison could look past the dog beside him and see the side of the mountain behind them.

In a quiet voice, Jamison began to explain to Jack what an avalanche was, how suddenly a sound in the wilderness snapped, how the layer under the surface of the fallen snow slipped, shifted, and slid and with it the overlying snow blanket. A measure of the size of the avalanche was how thick and heavy was that overlying blanket, which would fall in a rush, covering everything in its path and below: trees, rocks, animals, and man if he were stupid or unlucky enough to be in its angry way.

Jack looked at his master with loving eyes. He had feared two things: that his master had left him and that he might be alone here.

He had never been without a man to feed and protect him. This, he knew, was the difference between him and Army, Amee Lou, Sut, and the other dogs he had known. They seemed to know their dependence on loved or hated men. Jack did not know that there could be an invisible bond between dogs and men in the North Country, as if the tiniest thread connected them, which the wild raw whiteness was always striving to sever.

Jamison continued to talk. Jack felt his breath and knew this was the same kind of voice as the man who had loved him before. Jack London had talked to him like this, softly, a hand deep in his fur, kindly for such a rough place. Jack hoped never to be parted from Jake Jamison, this man he had saved from the white monster.

32

JACK LONDON IS HOLDING a photograph taken in the North Country.

Though he had never seen a person with a camera while he was in the Yukon, pictures had been taken and brought south to help people see and understand the Gold Rush.

How, thought London, can such a time and place be understood? How can I create timeless pictures on a page with only words?

How he wished he had a picture of Jack, the dog he had known on Split Up Island. Yet something was coming together in his imagination. Photograph or not, he was beginning to see it.

THE DOG AND THE man had been moving easily along the bottoms of valleys for days. The calm after the great fear of digging Jamison out of the small avalanche was soothing. The simple everyday life of waking and walking and eating and sleeping felt like a blessing for them both. Jack thought that it was possible that life would not always be covered with white, that other colors of life might be possible.

In the quiet, Jack began to notice birds. He was drawn first to the color of their feathers. He had never noticed small birds before. Small meant that should he wish to eat these birds, one of them would fit nicely in his mouth. Some of these birds had blue feathers, others were yellow. Jack wondered if they were called something. Jack had a name. Did they?

Now in this peaceful time they seemed to come to him, as if they had a message. Yet strain as he might, he could not understand their high chirping. There were clusters of them, and they settled in small trees along the trail. They chattered at each other, and often it seemed that they also chattered at him. Suddenly, without reason, a cluster of them would inhabit a whole tree; then they would unsettle themselves and fly around the tree or sometimes inside the tree—how could they do that? wondered Jack—and then settle again. Birds were quite mysterious.

33

◆} WHEN THEY MADE CAMP for the night, they put most of their effort into cooking, which in dead of winter was a greater chore than when dry firewood lay around for the taking, when they could camp by a stream and have running water, when the very ground was soft. Jack saw that he could be helpful by collecting wood for the fire the way Jamison showed him. Nuzzle it up with your muzzle and hold onto it with your jaws until you

could drop it by the campfire Jamison had kindled. Jack had to take care not to singe his fur. He was afraid of fire, so this was hard for him.

If Jamison talked to Jack, it would be after the setting up of the camp, after the evening meal, when what little of the sun was long gone, when they were settled in the tent. Jamison had been particularly quiet that day, no idle talk while walking.

The only event had been seeing a pack of wolves pass near their trail. The wind had been favorable, so the wolves had neither seen their tracks nor caught their scent. The moment he saw them, Jamison hunched down and tapped Jack lightly on the nose. They watched the wolves cross what in spring would have been a wide and lovely meadow. A small stream threaded its way across the valley like white lace.

After the wolves passed out of sight, sound, and scent, Jamison stayed staring after them. Jack whined softly but went unheard. Finally, Jamison rose and began walking the trail, not even looking alongside for Jack. They passed the remainder of daylight in this fashion, as if on two separate trails.

Now, resting on skins with only candlelight, Jamison looked at Jack and began to speak. Jack sensed immediately that there was a different tone in the

34

man's voice. Its timbre was deep and quiet, as if filtered through a wool scarf.

"I had another dog once. Great like you, my friend. Strong like you, and large. Not like you, he was an "insider" dog, of husky stock, though I never saw his mother or litter. This was north of Dawson City two years ago, before the gold strike, when the land was not infested with greedy men."

Jack perked his ears and strained to understand the man's tone. He shifted his paws and inched closer.

"One day we were upside of the mountain, he and I—I called him Prince 'cus he liked to prance a bit and always held his head high. Our attention was caught downslope by jus' such a pack o' wolves like we saw today. Difference was, that day the wind was off toward us and they caught our scent right away. Sun was high 'n they turned direction and took some toward us, as if we were odd, you know?"

Jack did not know, but he sensed that Prince and his master had been in danger. He whined, and Jamison reached to touch him.

"Imagine what we looked like to the passing stranger above? A pack o' wolves, a man and his dog lookin' at each other like there was something new to see. Nope, they had seen the likes of us and we of them . . . but not this sort of patient lookin', you know?"

Jamison did not wait for Jack but continued his far-off look. "The leader moved back through the pack and grabbed the shoulder of one of the wolves and pulled him forward to be out in the clear ahead of where the pack settled. The leader stood there with his brother and watched us. I wasn't sure what I was supposed to do. I had never seen wild animals act this way, but I stood up, really without thinkin', and began to walk toward the two of them."

Jack began to tremble, not knowing why. Jamison put a second hand on him. "Won't hurt you, boy, won't, I promise." He was quiet for several minutes, until Jack stopped shaking.

35

"As I walked toward the leader and his mate, the others in the pack were unsettled. I guess I could feel that because so was I unsettled. Finally, I was within a stroke of the leader and his mate. I stopped. The leader waited and then nudged the other wolf toward me. That wolf whined and tried to turn away from me, but the leader nipped his haunches. Bit by bit, the shy wolf and I came close enough to touch. I looked at him, but he had no eyes. I know not how such a thing could be, but his eye sockets, if they had ever been there, were covered by a thick layer of fur. He was surely blind. He was thin for a wolf in this country. There had been plenty of game that winter, no one went hungry but this fellow. I kneeled down 'side him and touched his fur, which was strangely soft. As I did that, the pack came agitated and began movin' around, as if they didn't know which way to go."

Jack felt sad. He could tell by Jamison's voice that something was going to happen—he remembered his friends, those left behind with the bad brothers, those who were hurt. Jack looked at Jamison and waited.

"I looked at the leader of wolves, wishing that critter could talk and tell me what he wanted of me. But he could not, yet he got up off his haunches and nudged the blind wolf toward me again, as if he wanted his brother wolf to go with me. After a while, I knew that this wolf leader wanted me to take his mate with me and my dog an' leave these parts. I looked back at Prince as if I wanted him to say something. He was a husky, wasn't he? He must know what these others were sayin' to me. Quick like, he jumped up and began trotting toward me. Then it all happened."

Jack whined louder now, as if to tell his master something the other dogs had not told him. Jamison was hypnotized by his own story and could not stop. "The pack leaped toward us. The first five to reach where I was with the pack leader and the blind wolf ran clean past me and attacked Prince. It was such a surprise, you know, that neither of us were prepared nor knew

36

what to do. I had a rifle back with my gear beside Prince, but it was too late to reach it. Five wolves attacked Prince, and he went down quick. The rest of the pack tried to get to me, but the leader and the blind wolf stayed with me and fought them off. One bad 'un got behind me for a moment until the blind wolf turned on him as if he could see and ripped off his ear. I looked behind me, and Prince was lyin' in the snow soaked in blood. The pack had stopped stock still now and was howlin' at their leader and the blind wolf. The leader would make small leaps forward to nip a pack member and then leap back aside me."

37

"I had nothing to help me, but the leader who I thought might yet feed me to his mates, but then, hadn't he fought off his own pack to keep me whole? It was a standoff. The pack sensed it and backed away, leavin' me with the blind animal and the leader, who nudged my leg as if to say 'go now.' He turned to lead the pack away from me. They followed him, and I ran back to Prince to see if I could save him." Jamison stopped and looked away from Jack. "But I couldn't save him. He was dead. In a minute. They had got to his throat, and he was a goner. I turned to look back behind me, and the pack was nowhere to be seen. Gone in a minute. But there by my own rig was the blind wolf gazing at me as if he could see. Sitting as if waitin' for supper, or for a pat on the head. He knew my dog was down and began to lick the blood off his neck as if to bring him back to life. . . ."

Jack crept forward until his muzzle lay in the man's lap, and they both stayed there without saying a word for what seemed like a long long time. Then they fell asleep.

❧ RAGINGLY AWAKE, JACK LONDON is deep in the writing of a book about dogs and men in the Yukon. A full novel it will be, not a short story like the others. The images of his time in the great white silence flood his brain, often to overflowing, until his hand falters on the page and he sorts through this story heard at the fire on Split Up Island, that story heard in Dawson having a hard drink, and yet another about men passing through ragged land caught on the edge of a small river in the wild whiteness. The stories seemed to stack themselves like delicious pancakes in his mind. Yet when his pencil falters, the details of the men, their dogs, and the rawness of the white silence sort themselves out and flow smoothly onto the pages until his weary head falls on the writing table, dead asleep.

Then he dreams about men lighting fires, about the hunger for gold, or about a simple hot meal, or about Jack, the dog he knew in the North Country. What, he wonders in his dream, happened to Jack?

THE STORY OF THE dog who dug his master out of an avalanche made the rounds of campfires in the North Country. Old grizzled hands also scoffed openly of the stupidity of a man traveling alone in this country with only one dog.

But then other stories began to be told of this same dog saving others in larger and more dangerous avalanches. Jack built a small name for himself around campfires where men drank the strong black liquid.

Avalanche Dog, they called him. It was a new idea to them, a dog that could sniff out a person buried deep in the snowpack.

No one knew how many men were lost to the oceans of snow that fell during the winter. Counting was fruitless, and the lives of men often didn't count for much anyway. It was a time when there were too many men in the Yukon for all the wrong reasons, reasons that did not have to do with caring for others who might be lost to an avalanche, or to the bitter cold when heat was mostly just an idea in a man's mind. This dog who could save a person became special in a way that was newly recognized in the North Country.

Jack often wondered what his old friend Jack London might think of his new small fame, a dog's own gold lode.

WHEN THEY WERE HIGH in a pass or along the tops of mountains, Jack might see a village below. Small cabins often appeared by a small stream. There might be movement. Men with dogs hauled heavy sleds with provisions—food, lumber, supplies brought from the larger towns near larger rivers.

They never went down into these places. Why is that? wondered Jack. When he was on Split Up Island, they went to Dawson for goods and supplies. Why not into these smaller towns? Often he looked at Jamison to see if the man was looking down into the village.

Once, on a ridge top, they stopped to rest. On one side was one of these villages, on the other a view into the mountains. Jack noticed that Jamison sat looking away from the cabins, while Jack wanted to watch to see if there were something he had not seen before.

What an odd sight, thought Jamison. I am looking in one direction, and my dog is looking in another, yet we are sitting here together, shoulder to haunch. Odder still that often he wished to be with other people, and he thought the dog preferred to be away from places like the village below. Jamison could not know Jack's longing for new smells, like the horses in Dawson and the different smells of men and their buildings. Yet they continued to sit together yet apart in such moments.

IT WAS ANOTHER WHITE day. They walked on snow. There was always snow above them now on the mountaintops, yet neither dog nor man could see the tops because of dense white clouds massed above. It had been that way for days. Jamison kept looking up, as if he were expecting something. And then it came.

It began with what Jack thought sounded like a gunshot. He had once been where a man held something like a stick, and it had made this hard booming sound. Jamison stopped and backed up some steps. Jack followed. As they looked up, a thin cracking line ripped through the side of the mountain valley ahead of them. It was impossible to tell if the crack was in the white sky or in the snow on the side of the mountain. Then the side of the mountain began to rain down, ten or twelve feet of snow, a small mountain of its own, coming down the steep valley ahead of them as if white fragments of the sky were falling on the land. Jack could feel the wind making its way over to where he and Jamison stood. What must have been the force of that

40

wind in the midst of the avalanche? Jack sensed Jamison's body relaxing. Though the wind might touch them, the falling snow and breaking timber would not; they were away from it, safe. Now they could watch what happened at a distance and count their good luck.

Jamison closed his eyes, and his head jerked up. He seemed to feel it, he thought, only because he had been under the smaller one that Jack had saved him from. Had they been three hundred yards farther along the trail, they would surely have perished, man and dog, beneath an ocean of whiteness. Bless us, gods of the trail, we are safe for one more day, prayed Jamison.

The snow formed a white tongue, lashing down the slopes driven by the wind as if the wind itself was after something or someone, though there was no person or animal to be seen. The tongue hesitated and transformed itself to a billowing balloon and danced down the slope, lightly, as if to tease, before becoming a rain of icicles hurtling over hillocks and rises in the mountainside, only to come together again and remake itself into an ocean determined to flood the world.

Jack's ears lay flat, as if he could feel the white storm even at this distance. He looked up at Jamison, who seemed equally dazed by the sight. Jamison looked down at Jack and said, "The French word for avalanche means to swallow. . . . look there, friend, at how it swallows the land, and how fortunate we are to be here, not there. That's how close a fella can be to the end of the trail."

Jamison patted the dog and closed his eyes. "Think about it this way, Friend Dog, what you just saw took less time than to stir a mug of coffee . . . or blow your nose, eh."

WORDS TUMBLE FROM THE man, leaking out the stubs of pencils, all from feverish memory. During the seven months Jack London spent in the wild gold country he made no notes, wrote no letters, kept no journals or

42

diaries. All his writing comes from the memory of men and dogs, a memory as vast as the North Country itself. This intuitive mind drives the man and his pencils.

The stack of pages on the desk grows into its own white mountain. The pages now have a title: Call of the Wild. It will be a story of a dog stolen from the south, brought to the Yukon, and sold into a kind of brutal animal slavery. But this dog is different. His fate will be . . . well, the story will tell itself when it is finished.

Jack London writes on and on. . . . His goal is to write one thousand words each day, no matter what!

❧ WIND TORMENTED THE SMALL tent. They were higher now and near a pass. Elements clashed together. Jack's ears pricked, and he raised his head. He heard a sound beyond the wind. He looked over at Jamison, but what caught his attention was something wilder than the wind at the tent flap. Instinctively Jack rose and flung himself at whatever that wild thing might be. It was soft, and he knocked it over easily. There was a scream and a scuffle, and Jamison was up now, yelling—yelling at whatever it was, trying to talk to Jack within the blackness of the tent. Another scream, and this time Jamison knew it was a woman.

How could there be a woman here?

"Do you have the Avalanche Dog? Where is he? They said they saw him near here—Jesus save a sinner, mister, do you have him?"

Calm arrived when Jamison settled Jack down, speaking softly to him, at the same time eyeing the woman's outline at the opening of the tent. He lit a candle and she became visible. She had wild hair like a witch, a shapeless dress that reached to her feet, and silver bracelets that caught the candlelight. They stood there like statues, staring at each other.

"Well," she said. Her eyes dropped, and she looked at Jack.

"Is that him?"

"Yes, ma'am," said Jamison.

Though it was still night, her story was clear as day. Each one of them—man, woman, and dog—played the tale she told them over in their minds as they struggled over the pass and down the slopes into the scooped valley below. Signs of the recent avalanche were everywhere: trees shredded to spaghetti or just littering the terrain like broken matchsticks, rocks thrown like children's balls, large gaps in the flow of the terrain, the land itself uprooted.

The woman's girl-child, some nine years old, became lost in this white sea. It was not clear to Jamison how this had happened, but it had, and the woman said she and her child were the only human things there. Snow is always deciding either to soften into water or harden into crystal, and if it becomes hard, it does so quickly. Everything had changed.

At one point, the going was so slow in the deep snow that the woman, in her fear of losing the child, tried to pick Jack up and carry him with a strength she did not have. The dog and the woman flailed in the snowpack. She dropped Jack and shoved him ahead of her, yelling at him. She wanted to fly

44

over the snowpack to reach where the child had been lost. Nothing, it seemed, would allow them to soar over the snow, beyond the pass. It was easy for Jamison to be patient, as he came to respect the courage and determination of the woman to get them to the spot, if it could be found, where the girl-child might be buried. It seemed a hopeless task in the eerie, moonlit night.

Finally the woman stopped and pointed to the left and downslope. "There," she said. "It was there!"

Edges of moonlight revealed a sea of snow as large as a small village littered with broken trees and slabs of hardened snow breaking up the landscape.

"She went down there."

Jack moved forward to let his nose catch the wind, which was blowing toward them, so that what was there might be known to his nose. Then he lowered his head to catch a scent over the snow, reaching to sense what might be underneath.

JACK LONDON FEELS A wildness in himself, and he almost dances before his wife, Charmain. She watches him with concern while she prepares a meal for them in their house in Oakland.

He has sent the manuscript of his new full-length novel to the East, to his publisher, Macmillan, in New York, in hope of a quick response. London paces and runs a hand through his hair. He sits and then suddenly stands to walk again. He cannot be still.

"I hope it's not too short. Twain writes short things, but Dickens is voluminous, and now I am in between."

"It will be all right, Jack, they will see how exquisitely you have captured the wild North and the inner life of dog and man," she said.

"I so hope, I so hope . . ."

"Come, I have made us a meal."

45

THE WOMAN PULLED A cloth sack from under her dress. The bag was tied tightly by a small rope, which she untied. She upended it onto the snow in front of Jack. Clothes. Child's clothes. A small yellow dress, hair ribbon, hair brush and comb, a tiny handkerchief, another ribbon, red that caught the light of the moon.

Jack sniffed the clothes. Jamison looked on with wonder in his eyes at the shrewd intelligence of the woman to bring the scent of the child to the dog, as if knowing instinctively that might be the only life ring for the girl-child. Jack sniffed deeply, as if he knew what he had to do. He had become Avalanche Dog, and this was his greatest test. He looked up at Jamison and whined. Jake Jamison knelt down in the snow, put his hands deep into the dog's fur, and spoke to him softly. The dog whined again, looked up at the woman with her desperate eyes flashing at him, and strode off into the snow-pack, nose to the snow.

Jamison and the woman let the dog lead, staying behind him and upwind so as not to distract him. The woman looked at Jamison and said, "I have never felt as helpless in my life." Jamison looked at her. She was younger than he had thought and perhaps more beautiful than the wild-eyed screaming woman who had burst into their tent. He saw longing for the child in her eyes and watched her sure step as they followed the dog downslope. They were careful to step around or over the chaos of rocks and broken timber from the avalanche that littered the landscape.

The wind shifted and was suddenly behind Jack. He stopped, confused for a moment, and turned to look at Jamison. Then he ran downslope over the snowpack until he was a dark speck far away, but then he turned, suddenly coming back uphill toward them, led by his nose into the wind and to the ground below. Clearly, the senses of the dog were trying to go below the snow, to periscope down and down. The woman and Jamison stood their ground and watched. Jack wove back and forth over the slope. He did this for

46

two hundred yards and then sat down and looked up at the moon. The silent, wild country, it seemed, cared not for the life of the girl-child lost within.

They did not move while Jack sat. Suddenly, he was up again, digging into the snowpack. Jamison and the woman raced downslope to see if the dog had found her. Jamison wondered about the depth of the snow there; the woman stopped to collect pointed tree limbs as large as clubs.

When they were almost within reach of Jack, he jerked up with something in his mouth and began to howl at the moon. The woman slowed to approach Jack, not to startle him, and reached out her hand.

Jack dropped a small knitted glove into her hand. Jamison fell to his knees, digging. "My God, save us, is she there?" the woman asked.

Seconds became minutes before Jamison's head came out of the snow. The man looked around the hole for the dog. Neither the woman nor Jamison

47

had noticed that Jack was circling the find, first with nose upslope and then downslope, around and around while the woman cried into the frozen mitten until it softened. Jamison went to her and pulled her up and held her in his arms." Wait, wait … it's not over. Watch Jack, jes' watch." He turned her round and round, twisting them into the snowpack, so she could watch Jack circle the find.

"You haven't told us her name."

Being held by Jamison was the first moment of warmth the woman had experienced since her child had become lost in the avalanche. That seemed to have happened months ago, yet here she was looking over the man's shoulder at the dog circling and circling, trying to teach himself where the girl-child might be.

She could not take her eyes from the red mitten, which she held high at Jamison's shoulder so she would not lose sight of it. It was proof of life, though that life was still buried in the snowpack. But the fact of the mitten allowed her to see, actually feel, her daughter in other past times, as when they had been together on a summer day in Fairbanks. They had passed a candy store on the street, and the child had begged for candy in the way a child does. The woman heard the child's voice as though it were that particular day and they were safe. She added her own current "please" to the begging, as if her Lord could hear her and this was her last chance to gain His attention and His will to save the child. Please, God . . . I gave the child candy that day, I was a good mother then and am so now, can I have my own candy child now, please, Lord. . . .

She felt Jamison's arms again, and it brought her mind back to the mountainside. He was looking at her. From a far distance she could hear Jamison say something, what was it?

"You haven't told us the name of your girl-child."

The woman looked up into Jamison's eyes and answered, "Clemmie . . .

48

Clementine." It seemed to Jamison in that moment that the woman could actually see the child, running freely along the valley, free of the avalanche, running free as a nine-year-old child should to embrace the country that was her home. Yet, a child cannot know of danger until it grips her arm like a scolding parent. The woman was not like that—she was simply unaware of the dangers that came with living in a small village here in the Yukon, where death was invisible until its fatal moment. A crack in the wild—what might that mean? And before the meaning is clear, the white mountain was over you like a chilling blanket, never to be warm again.

Before they knew it, Jack was loping back downslope, beyond where he had gone downhill when the wind shifted. Jamison and the woman watched him slow, stop, and then come back up the mountain toward them.

The woman looked into Jamison's eyes with wonder and fear.

Jack looked upslope and saw two silhouettes coming toward him. He moved from one place where the scent was fine and good to another and yet another. Again he looked up the mountain and saw his master and the crying woman coming toward him as fast as the snowpack would allow.

Jamison heard Jack's high soft howl. Jake felt the dog's dilemma.

They could see three places where he had settled, sniffed, lowered his nose as if to pierce the snowpack, and then move to the next spot.

Jamison decided to take matters into his own hands and unsheathed his small camp spade. He walked to one of the spots and began to dig. From another spot, Jack watched him, as if the man were another dog looking for his own bone.

Jack got up and moved to where Jamison was digging. He stuck his nose in the broken snow, breathed deeply, and then moved away to watch the man dig. The woman saw this indecision and wondered how this would return her daughter to her. She began to cry again, and breathed deeply, as if she too were trying to sniff out the right place.

49

Suddenly, Jack shifted to the third spot and punched his nose into the snow. He raised his head and began to howl loudly, as if to reach all the way to the

moon, which seemed to draw closer to look more deeply into this human dilemma. Jamison moved quickly to where Jack sat and began to draw a circle in the snow. He stood back for a moment to examine the circle. He looked at Jack. As if the dog agreed with the size of the circle, he jumped forward and began to dig a hole in the snowpack with his windmill force. The woman marveled at the flying paws and then produced one of the jagged branches. She pounded the point furiously into the circle's edge to loosen the snow so dog and man could move faster and deeper. Jamison completed the team, whirling his camp spade.

The spot Jack selected had one difference from the other two. There were jagged slabs of snowpack sticking up out of the earth where a tree had been snapped in half by the force of the wind, so that the bottom half of the tree was ripped away from the ground at the edge of their circle and the top half blown away downslope.

If the moon could have spoken that night, she would have said she had never seen such a sight—two humans and one animal digging into the earth as if they could create a tunnel to the bottom of the world. It was not long before the two humans were covered with sweat, chilling their faces. They wondered when they should dig furiously and when they should slow down and dig carefully in case the child might be near. The woman didn't understand that the slabs of snow tossed together created pockets of air within the snowpack. That both helped and hindered their digging, but if the child was in an air pocket, that might allow her to breathe long enough to be found alive. Jamison and the woman kept looking to Jack. His nose seemed to reach into the slabs and snowpack itself. Finally he slowed, and they did as well, until . . .

. . . a human cry was heard. For an instant, the woman thought it came from behind her. Jamison slowed his digging. Jack barked at them fiercely. . . be careful digging, he seemed to say, as he poked around a slab and into the snow as deftly as he could.

The sound seemed to be a voice from heaven to the woman. Her girl-child was alive, but how alive remained to be seen. Jack moved to the center of the hole and began to paw softly, as Jamison had seen him do before. He joined the dog and did the same, softly, softly, until he worked around a slab of snow and, in the smallest pocket between slabs, saw the shape of an ear, then some frozen hair, and finally an emerging face. The woman leaped for her child, and Jamison had to pull her away until Jack cleared enough of the snow from around the shape for them to pull the child safely up and out.

Jamison could see now that the girl had intuitively done what was necessary to survive an avalanche—she had tried to "swim" in the falling snow, creating a small air pocket that allowed her to breathe shallowly between the snow slabs and tree roots when she was finally encased in the frozen snow. There was no "ice mask" over her face, as when a person falls into the snow and does not move his or her face into an air space. These were saving graces.

Jamison took off his coat and laid it on the snowpack, and placed the girl-child on top of it. He instructed the woman to massage the limbs, to stroke them as softly as possible to encourage the blood back to where the cold had driven it away. Jack sat aside, looking in turns at the woman, at the girl-child he had saved, and at his master. Now his master knew what to do.

51

The girl's face was turned toward Jack. There were few children in the gold country. Jack had never seen a person that small and frail; she seemed a small wonder to him.

Finally she spoke.

"Who is that?" she asked her mother as she looked at Jack, who was now whining softly again.

"That is Jack, the Avalanche Dog. He is our new friend. He saved your life."

The woman turned swiftly to Jack, startling him. She threw her arms about the dog and whispered into his large ear warm words from her warm breath. "God be praised," said the woman. "You have let my child breathe again."

The dog pulled away. Jack was not used to women. He had never been held by one before, and they smelled different. While Jamison and the woman wrapped the girl-child in their coats to go downslope, Jack sat apart from them and watched the moon, which was always looking down on him and, tonight, smiling.

❧ THEY WERE SITTING ON a bench in Oakland, looking at San Francisco Bay and the city behind it. The moon shone over the city, the Bay, and Jack London and his wife. He took the folded Western Union telegram out of his breast pocket. He read it again to his wife, who sat beside him with her arm over his shoulder.

The telegram said:

```
Mr. London STOP We wish to publish your novel,
Call of the Wild  STOP Can you come to our offices
in New York to discuss terms, conditions and
remuneration STOP We await your reply   STOP
(signed)
Macmillan Publishers
```

Her eyes glistened as she beheld him. They looked at each other for a long time and then at the moon. They laughed at their good fortune.

❧ THE BRIGHT AFTERNOON SUN flowed through the windows of the woman's tiny cabin in the small village. This sun warmed the pile of animal and human bodies on rugs, skins, and blankets flooding the floor.

In the middle of the pile lay the girl-child, Clemmie, and beside her, the hero of the night, Jack the Avalanche Dog. Wrapped around them were the woman on one side and Jake Jamison on the other. All were deep in the sleep of life—life saved, life loved, life that is so fragile.

53

❧ FROM THIS TIME ON, Jack was known throughout the Yukon as Avalanche Dog, the dog who could dig life out of the moving mountains of avalanches.

He belonged to two men—the reality of Jake Jamison and the memory of Jack London.

A 1903 quotation from the Oakland Times:

> "with the publishing of *Call of the Wild*, a book that is certain to become the leading myth of the Rush for Gold and Life in the White Wilderness, our neighbor, Jack London, has become America's leading novelist, known and written about in cities and towns all the way across America to New York, the home of his famous publisher, Macmillan, who bought the book rights for the grand sum of $2,000.00.
> We salute Jack London."

What the Oakland Times did not mention in 1903 is that memory is indestructibly lodged in our hearts. It is this memory that connects us, no matter the distance or time.

We are memory and memory is us.

❧ TWO DAYS AFTER THE avalanche, they were mostly recovered. Jamison said he was going over the mountain for a few days. He realized that this would not be a good time to take Jack with him, because Clemmie was not ready to give up her new friend and savior. Jamison took Clemmie's mother aside and told her his plan. For a moment, Jamison thought she would ask to go with him. She paused, cleared her throat, looked down at her bracelets, and then gazed back at Jamison. "You'll be careful, right?"

Jamison paused and then nodded.

54

The woman looked deeply into Jamison's blue eyes and said, "You'll come back here, right?"

Jamison nodded and smiled at her.

It was harder to make Jack understand that he was not going over the mountain. Jamison had to make several attempts to leave without him. He would set out and then, finding the dog beside him again, turn back to Clemmie and have her hold Jack beside her. After fifteen minutes, Jack understood and sat beside the child and whined softly as Jamison left. He was his master and friend. They had been together. Jack did not want to lose him like he had lost his good friend Jack London. Clemmie whispered into Jack's ear, "He is coming back to us." She patted the dog's head. "Don't worry, its jus' a day or so."

Jamison disappeared, and Clemmie pulled Jack inside the tiny cabin and by the fire. "Look," she said to the dog. "I can read." Her head lifted and she seemed proud for a moment. At that moment her mother came in to watch them. "The dog don't know most child'rn can't read, 'specially girl child'rn." Clemmie nodded. Jack's ears perked. He lay down at Clemmie's feet, head up and ready to be read to.

Because dogs can't read and don't understand books and, most important, because no one had ever read to Jack before, it was a new experience. Clemmie lay down in front of the fire and read in his ear a storybook her mother had brought from St. Louis, Missouri, where they lived before. There they had a real library, and Clemmie could borrow books. Neither the woman nor Clemmie explained these things to Jack because he was asleep before she could read five pages.

When Jack woke up, Clemmie was curled with him, a blanket over her shoulders. He had difficulty being around the woman—she smelled different—but the child smelled right to Jack, so he was content to be that close to her. Later they both got up. Jack went to the door and nosed it open to go outside to see if Jamison had returned. He whined until Clemmie came outside to stand with him. She wondered what she could do to calm the dog and maybe distract him. Suddenly she had an idea and went inside to ask her mother if she could go down to the village and take Jack with her. Yes, she could.

The cabin sat alongside a tiny trickle of a stream that was good for drinking and cooking water but for little else. The girl and the dog walked along the stream to a small bridge that led to a group of cabins like the one they had just left. There were teams of dogs, which caught Jack's eye right away. Clemmie steered him toward a cabin with a porch and an open door that led into a store.

They went inside.

Several men sat around a large potbellied black stove. They were smoking pipes and talking loudly. The moment Clemmie approached with Jack, one of the men turned to her and asked if that was THE dog. She nodded shyly and stood right beside Jack. The man got up and walked over to examine Jack. The dog was uncertain what would happen and backed up a step.

56

"I won't hurt ya," the man said. "I never saw such a dog."

"He's a Southlander," said another man. All the men nodded then.

"How do ya suppose he learned that?" said a third man. "I mean 'ta dig a person outta the avalanche?"

Clemmie smiled and said, "It's his nose, he has a good sense that can sniff out anything." The men regarded her. She was the only child within a hundred miles of where they were. No one brought children to the Yukon, so she was a curiosity, though she did not know that. She stood up to the man who had asked about Jack and nodded. "He is a special dog, and I know that one day people will find out and he will be famous."

The standing man smiled broadly at her gumption. He nodded, "Ya know, little lady, I'll bet a turnip yur right 'bout that. Folks will find out 'bout yur dog and say nice things, 'cause he did save yur life and that's a hero dog, I'd say." The other men nodded as if he had said something wise, and pulled on their pipes.

The man who owned the small store walked over to Clemmie and held out his hand with some colored sticks in it. "Like a 'spearmint stick, young lady?"

She smiled and reached slowly and delicately to take a 'spearmint stick. She curtsied at the owner man, who reached in his apron pocket and pulled out a morsel for Jack. The dog turned to the man as gently as Clemmie had, took the morsel in his mouth, and chewed. Clemmie curtsied to the store owner again. She turned to the other men to say, "You have been kind, gentlemen, but we must go home now. Thank you."

The gathering of men stood and gazed as if they were watching a princess in a fancy parade as the girl and the dog walked out of the store and back up to their cabin. Jack looked up at Clemmie and wondered if his life was changing now that he walked with a girl-child.

AFTERWORD

Who Was Jack London?

I have written this book in admiration of Jack London. As a writer, I have heroes, and he is one of mine. I am trying to be the storyteller he was as well as dig into the hearts and minds of men and animals. Fortunately, my love of nature and animals is as deep as his, so my "memory play" imagines the connections between Jack London and Jack, the dog of the North, who was one of his inspirations.

With the publishing of *Call of the Wild* in July 1903, Jack London became the most admired and popular author in America. He remained so until his early death at age forty in 1916. During his life, he wrote more than thirty-books. If what a writer is interested in can be determined by what he writes about, then we know he was fascinated by the lore of the North Country—the men and dogs who inhabited that raw land during the rush for gold.

We know that he traveled a great deal, so there are books about his travels.

What is not widely known is that Jack London was a Socialist. A Socialist then was a person concerned with the well-being of all people whatever their social or economic class. The book London published immediately after *Call of the Wild* was his first venture into his beliefs as a Socialist. *The People of the Abyss* was about the poor people of London, England and their social and economic plight. This was followed by similar books such as *War of the Classes* and *The Iron Heel,* and others. Clearly the ideas he expressed in these books were inspirational. Even though he was considered a great man and writer, he never lost interest or faith in the common man. His work was considered a revolutionary call to the human soul, especially to youth and their search for justice.

A good example of this call is found in a letter to him from a European youth who said, "I have just read my first Jack London book, *Call of the Wild*. Your thoughts in this book mean everything to me: adventure, courage, the importance of humanistic ideas, the devastation of hunger, and the willingness to stand up for who you are and what you believe for your life."

In other words, for all of us, no matter our age, Jack London and his writings are a call to live life to the fullest. London himself said:

> *I would rather be ashes than dust! I would rather*
> *that my spark should burn out in a brilliant blaze*
> *than it should be stifled by dryrot. I would rather*
> *be a superb meteor, every atom of me in magnificent*
> *glow, than a sleepy and permanent planet.*
>
> *The proper function of man is to live,*
> *not just to exist. I shall not waste my days*
> *trying to prolong them. I shall use my time.*

Who was Jack London? A man larger than life itself, who created himself through his writing and ideas without the benefit of the media blitz that attends the life of any writer or celebrity today. Here is a man who, one hundred years later, stands proudly alone on his body of work as an American hero.

60

❧

JACK LONDON'S DOG
was designed and illustrated by Barry
Moser in the summer and autumn of 2007. The
type is Bembo, a typeface that was designed by
Stanley Morison and appeared in 1929 from the Lanston
Monotype corporation in England. It was based on a typeface
that was originally designed and cut by Francesco Griffo. His types
were first printed in February 1495 in a book entitled DE AETNA, a
short text recounting a journey to Mount Aetna that was written by then
Italian Cardinal Pietro Bembo. ❧ The illustrations are relief engravings, a
printmaking technique in which the image is drawn onto, and then cut into
hard, end-grain boxwood with very sharp gravers. Today Moser cuts his images
into a wood-substitute material called Resingrave (a cast polymer resin) that
was invented by Richard Woodman in Redwood City, California in 1989. It
is an extraordinarily difficult (albeit it simple in principle) printmaking medi-
um to master wherein the white lines and areas are cut away leaving the
black lines and areas standing. The blocks are then printed on a printing
press and the proofs are scanned and dropped into the text to be repro-
duced. ❧ The book was printed & bound in China by AsiaPacificOffset. ❧
The illustrator would like to thank Miss Ava Harper for her good
work posing as Clemmie, and his good dog Ike, an English mas-
tiff (the largest breed of dog in the world) for his patience in
being photographed as the stand-in for Jack, the dog. His
footprint, carefully collected and engraved, is repro-
duced on the facing page at actual size.

❧